Disney's
My Very First Winnie the Pooh™

Roo's New Baby-sitter

Written by
Kathleen W. Zoehfeld

Illustrated by
Robbin Cuddy

SCHOLASTIC INC.

New York Toronto London Auckland Sydney
Mexico City New Delhi Hong Kong Buenos Aires

First published by Disney Press, New York, NY.
This edition published by Scholastic Inc., 90 Old Sherman Turnpike, Danbury, CT 06816
by arrangement with Disney Licensed Publishing.

ISBN 0-7172-8873-0

Printed in the U.S.A.

"Roo, dear, your baby-sitter will be here soon," said Kanga.

"I don't want to be baby-sitted!" cried Roo.

"Now, Roo. Mama's just going out for a little shopping and supper with Aunt Sadie," said Kanga. "You'll have fun with Pooh."

"I don't want to have fun," cried Roo. "I'm going SHOPPING. I can shop like anything."

"Yes, dear," said Kanga. She was busy buttoning her coat and looking for her purse.

Roo found a large bag and began filling it with things. "Look at me shopping!" he cried. "I'd be a BIG help shopping."

"Some other time, dear," said Kanga.

"What other time?" asked Roo.

"Well, not this time," said Kanga. "Oh, look! Here comes Pooh now."

"Hallo, Pooh," said Roo. "I'm shopping!" He put more cans in his bag, partly because this was fun, and partly because he didn't want his mama to see how much he minded being left behind.

"Pooh," said Kanga, "don't let Roo get into any mischief."

"Oh, I won't let him get into anything," said Pooh cheerfully.

"Bye-bye!" Roo and Pooh waved as they watched Kanga hop down the path and over the bridge. When she was out of sight, Roo drooped.

Pooh gave Roo a hug and put him in his high chair.

"What you need is a nice smackerel of honey to cheer you up," said Pooh.

"I like shopping," squeaked Roo. "I don't need to eat."

"Hmmmm, doesn't want to eat," said Pooh. "NOW what do I do?"

"You don't know how to baby-sit?" asked Roo.

"Well, yes," said Pooh, "all except the actual baby-sitting part."

"I'm good at baby-sitting," said Roo. "I'll tell you how."

"The first thing a baby-sitter does is play store," said Roo.

He showed Pooh how to set up the cash register and where to put all the toys and cans and bags.

When they were finished playing, Pooh sat down for a little rest.

"The next thing a baby-sitter does is climb!" cried Roo. "Let's see who can climb the highest, you or me."

Pooh, who was beginning to think there was not much SITTING involved in baby-sitting, said, "Okay, let's find a good climbing tree."

They stood under the old apple tree in
Roo's backyard. Roo jumped and jumped,
but he couldn't reach even the lowest branch.

"Baby-sitters always give a boost," he said.
"I see," said Pooh.

Roo hopped from
branch to branch, and Pooh
climbed up behind him.

"Mmmm," said Roo.
"Look at those apples.
Baby-sitters always pick
apples for supper."

Pooh clambered up to the highest branch.
He picked four bright red apples and tucked
them under his arm. Then he
inched back down.

"Oh, Pooh," cried Roo.
"You can climb with one arm!"

"Oops! I'm just that sort of…"
Thump! "…baby-sitter," shouted
Pooh, as he discovered a faster
way down to Roo's branch.

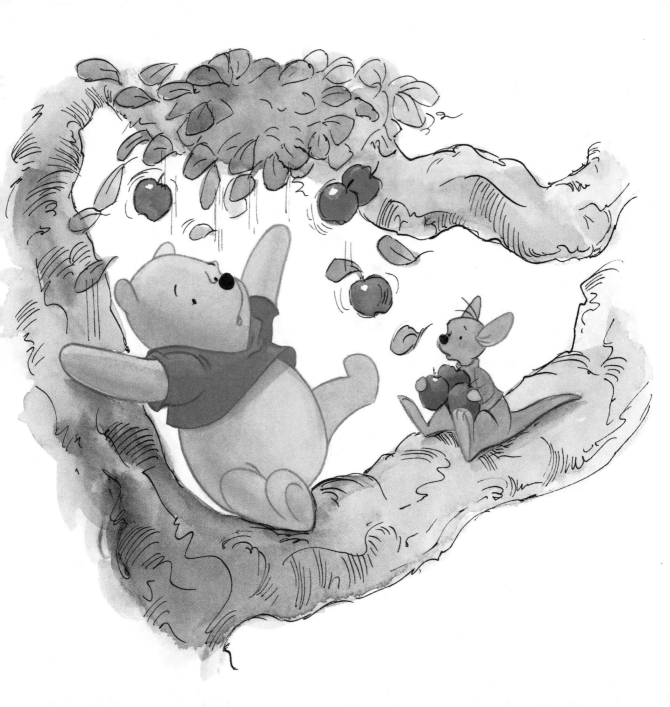

They sat side by side and swung their feet and ate the sweet apples.

"This is the best supper ever!" cried Roo.

"What do baby-sitters do AFTER supper?" asked Pooh.

"They give baths," said Roo, "with LOTS of bubbles."

Roo showed Pooh how baby-sitters pour a whole bottle of bubble bath into the bathwater.

"It seems like a lot," said Pooh.

"Just right," said Roo.

Roo took off his little vest and hopped in. He disappeared under the bubbles.

"Where's Roo?" asked Pooh, sort of to himself and sort of out loud. "Wfffffff." He blew on the bubbles. He couldn't see Roo anywhere.

He swished his paws through the bubbles. He couldn't feel Roo.

"Look at me jumping," squeaked a little voice. Pooh could HEAR Roo!

"There you are!" cried Pooh.

Roo, all wet and bubbly, was jumping on his bed.

Pooh chased him with the towel and rubbed him down. "Time for your Strengthening Medicine," said Pooh, a little more sternly than when Poohs usually say such things.

"I don't want it," said Roo. He folded his arms across his chest and stuck out his chin.

"Oh, well," sighed Pooh, slumping in a chair. "Why don't you give ME a spoonful? I think I could use it!"

"Now, Pooh, dear, here's your medicine," said Roo in a cheerful, grown-up sort of voice.

"Ahhh! Much better," sighed Pooh. "Thank you, Roo. You are a good baby-sitter."

"I'm baby-sitting!" sang Roo happily.